City, Sing for Me

A Country Child Moves to the City

by Jane Jacobson

Illustrated by Amy Rowen

Library of Congress Catalog Number 77-11130
ISBN: 0-87705-358-8
Copyright © 1978 by   Human Sciences Press
72 Fifth Avenue
New York, N.Y. 10011

Printed in the United States of America
89   987654321

Library of Congress Cataloging in Publication Data

Jacobson, Jane.
  City, sing for me.

  SUMMARY: Jenny is sad about moving from the country to the city until she
meets Rosa who shows her good times.
  [1. City and town life—Fiction. 2. Moving, House-
hold—Fiction] I. Rowen, Amy. II. Title.
PZ7.J1528Ci   [Fic]   77-11130

With Special Thanks to

Sam Reeves
Susannah Wilson
Philip Wilson
Marthe Rowen
Marc Cohen
Ron Judkoff

Jenny looked outside her window. She did not see sky. She did not see grass or flowers or trees.

Her family had just moved to the city from the country. Jenny grew up in the country. She had never been to a city before now.

Jenny crouched on the floor and turned her head almost backwards to look up; but she could not see sky. She climbed up on a chair and stuck her head out the window to look down; but she could not see trees or flowers or grass.

"I am nowhere;" Jenny thought.

All she saw was a brick wall and windows of the building built next to her building. Jenny was so close to the bricks outside her room that she saw each bump on each brick.

"Jenny, are you here?" her older brother Greg called.

"No I'm not." Jenny answered. She wished she was in the country still.

"So here you are." he said, coming into her room. "There are so many boxes piled up I couldn't find you. Let's leave all the mess a while. Mom and Dad said we could. They're busy with the movers."

Jenny shook her head, no. She had seen some of the city from car windows as her family drove there. The city looked ugly and scary.

"But don't you want to see where we live now?" Greg asked.

"I might feel better," Jenny thought, "if I see the sky."

Greg knew that Jenny was sad. He was sad too about moving from the country. But the city seemed exciting and fabulous like a monster.

"All right Greg. But let's go down the road only a little way. I'm afraid of getting lost." Jenny said.

"We don't live on a road anymore Jenny. We live on a street. Really we live on a block of a street." Greg said. He was three years older than Jenny. He liked to do crossword puzzles. "Each street has many blocks."

"One block then." Jenny frowned.

Together they scooted past the boxes. They squeezed past some movers who were trying to shove a long table around a tight corner. At last, they tumbled out the apartment door.

But they weren't outside yet.

They were in a hall with more shut doors than Jenny could count. Tiles in dingy black and white covered the floor. Everything was very straight and dark and square. Nothing was like the tree branches or clouds or new fallen snow that Jenny might see when she left her house in the country.

She heard no birds singing.

Jenny smelled paint and detergent and bug spray that all stung her nose. She got dizzy trying not to breathe too much or too deeply.

They waited for the elevator to come up to them. Jenny eyed the doors that surrounded them. Any stranger, or spook, might creep out of one of those doors. Her family did not know any neighbors. Jenny got more and more scared wondering who, or what, lived next door, down the hall, so close.

Jenny listened to the elevator coming. It clicked and whooshed and almost moaned. It sounded haunted.

"Let's walk to the street." Jenny said.

"It's too far." Greg said. He watched the numbers above the elevator glow green.

"No it's not." Jenny whispered. The elevator ghosts were coming nearer.

"We live twelve floors up." Greg said. "You can jump out the window tomorrow."

The elevator slid open. Greg stepped into its car. Jenny stayed in the hall.

"It's haunted. I'll get squished by the doors." Jenny said.

Somewhere behind her, Jenny heard a lock rattle and a door shake. Terrified, she glanced over her shoulder. The door swung open a crack; Jenny screamed. Without thinking anymore, she jumped into the elevator.

"Silly goose." Greg said.

She did not have time to worry who, or what, started to come after her upstairs. The elevator bumped to a stop. She charged out

so she couldn't be caught by the doors shutting.

But Greg and she still were not outside yet. They had to go through the lobby. No one sat on the chairs of this big, empty space. No one looked in the floor to ceiling mirrors. It was a place that belonged to everybody, where nobody stayed.

They pushed open the inside front door and, at last, the outside front door.

It was a hot August in the city. Jenny loved hot days in the country. A breeze always blew under a tree or by a stream to cool her. But, in the city, Jenny felt no breeze. The high walls of the buildings trapped the air. She felt sticky and steamy the minute she was outside her building.

She tilted her head back to see the square of blue sky and puff clouds. The buildings leaned over her. Her stomach felt sick. She closed her eyes.

Greg tugged her by the hand. He was talking. But Jenny could not hear him. The city noise thundered over his voice.

Jenny was sure there was no sound possibly louder than the city thunder she heard.

If there were birds singing, their songs could never reach her. Probably the birds didn't even bother singing, if there were birds.

Greg and Jenny went to the end of their block to a big, wide street that crossed their street. The noise from this wide street was louder than what Jenny had heard first. It was louder than loud. It was louder than Greg's shout which Jenny once believed was loudest of the loud.

Greg was shouting for her to stop. Jenny stood behind him on the curb. Cars screeched by them. Trucks growled. All the traffic pounded by them at once.

The noise made Jenny's teeth hurt, her elbows hurt. Smoke and fumes choked her. Her eyes burned. There was so much terrible waiting in the city.

The light on the wide street changed. A checkered taxi, a bus and a red car slammed to a halt along the crosswalk.

Crowds jostled Greg and Jenny. She was sure she'd be trompled. She wondered where all these people came from and where they were going. Both Greg and she were half carried, half dragged across the street by them.

"I've had enough!" Jenny shrieked to Greg, "It's one block."

They turned back to their new home.

No matter how hot the street was, the lobby of their building seemed damp and chill like the bottom of a well. Jenny shivered.

"I'll race you up the steps." Jenny said, scared of the elevator.

"It's not fair to you." Greg said, "My legs are longer." He didn't want to tell her how tired he felt.

"Well, I'll race the elevator then, it has no legs." Jenny wanted to get away. She wanted to be high above the street, crowds and lobby.

She beat the elevator.

Minutes later, Greg appeared. "An old lady and her three poodles had to get off on another floor. Otherwise I'd have been first."

"Storyteller."

"No, it's true. It's true it's a story." Greg tried to smile.

Jenny slipped into her room. She went to the window where her plant sat. "How will you grow?" she asked it, "There is so little light."

She spit on the leaves to wipe off the grime covering them already. "Please live," she said to it and began to cry. She let the tears drop on the plant so it could drink them.

Even though her room was dark, with the walls of other buildings so near, Jenny chose it. It was the quietest place to be found in the city.

Still, she heard a siren wail now. Someone played music like cats howling or maybe cats howled howls like music. It all made Jenny sadder. She cried till she believed her tears touched the plant's roots.

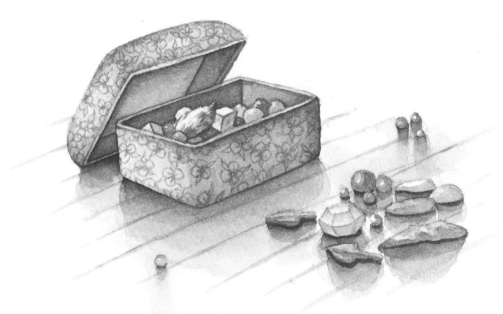

She tried wrapping her head in a blanket to keep out the sad noises. The noises became a low buzz. It was hot with a blanket around her head, so she lay on the floor. A little air stirred there.

Jenny had a treasure box she brought from the country. She did not let it be packed in the big boxes of everything. She pulled it out now from a corner of her closet. It was the only friendly thing, besides her plant, in an awful new place.

In the box, she saved rocks and special booty she collected while exploring the country. The city was one hard chunk of stone but there were no stones she could hold in her hand.

Her favorite was a meteorite that fell out of space. Jenny rubbed it with her fingers. When she grew up, she wanted to be an astronaut. She wanted to touch the moon.

She had sandstone that sparkled in the sun. "It's like stars inside earth," she thought. But now it was dull. Her glass prism did not make rainbows.

Jenny fell asleep imagining how the sandstone and prism used to shine. Stars in the daytime, in my hand. Sun a star too, yellow dwarf star, close to earth.

When Jenny woke, it was darker in her room. At first, she forgot where she was. She looked out the window. Squares of light floated out there all around her. She saw people in those windows.

"Everyone in the city," she thought, remembering where she was, "lives on top of each other. I am lost in a heap of people."

Jenny guessed it must be time for the first star to come out. She couldn't be sure though because she could not see the sky. She worried that she was going to have bad luck in the city.

"If I wish every other day for the star to be there the next day, and if it's there when I wish, then I'll have half as many wishes as in the country, but I'll be certain about them. That is if I wish when the star is there that the star is there. Oh no, it's useless."

"Star bright, star light, if you're up there now, I wish I may, I wish I might have the wish I wish tonight." She hoped it worked.

She unwrapped her head. In the country she knew where she was by the north star. She did not trust all the signs and numbers of the city.

Jenny heard a legend about the north star. American Indians said that once upon a time some hunters lost their way in the forest. They prayed that a path home might be shown to them. A little girl appeared. She was the spirit of the north star. She guided them home. When they grew old, the hunters wished to go to the north star where she lived in the little dipper.

Jenny wanted to be an astronaut from the moment she heard the legend. She wanted to go to the north star. She'd look down at earth. No one would ever be lost again.

The next day, Greg said, "We'll go farther than yesterday. We'll go to the park."

"How far is farther?" Jenny asked.

"Maybe five blocks." Greg said, wanting to sound brave.

Jenny thought "I might feel better if I see some trees and grass." But she didn't really want to be outside again. Any distance farther in the city was too far from the country.

Jenny and Greg looked both ways at the curb on the big street. Cars and buses and trucks were tearing by very fast. Greg perched at the edge of the curb. The light for the big street

traffic was green.

"Now, Jenny, run!" Greg yelled. Before Jenny blinked, he darted to the other side of the street. A car was honking. She tried to follow him. Another car honked. She was afraid she'd be hit.

"Scaredy-cat"; Greg hollered, "I'm not hanging around anymore. Go home where you belong." Greg was tired of helping Jenny be happy. He had to help himself be happy in the city. It was too hard to be happy for two.

Jenny was alone. She'd never been alone in a city. She didn't know where the park was. She started back the way her brother and she had come.

She could not remember which building was her building.

She swung open many big front doors and peeked into many gloomy front lobbies. Each one seemed very much like every other one.

Finally, she had to rest from swinging all those heavy doors. She sat down on the steps of one especially gigantic building. She decided to wait till she saw Greg coming home down the street. There was nothing else to do. She'd tried all the doors of all the buildings on her block.

"Hey, haven't I seen you around here before?" someone said. Jenny turned. A girl, about her size, was coming out of the gigantic building. She had thick curly hair.

"No you haven't seen me. I'm lost. I haven't been around anywhere."

"You just moved here yesterday, right?" the girl asked, putting her hands in her pockets.

"How do you know?" Jenny asked, amazed that anyone would notice someone as small as she was in a city as big as the city was. "I just moved from the country."

"And you live in that building over there, right?" The girl pointed to a building directly across the street.

Jenny looked at the building. She was astonished that this girl could tell the difference between one building and another. She was more astonished that this girl might know where she lived.

The building did seem familiar. It had flowers cut out of stone under the windows. She liked those flowers when she first saw them yesterday.

"I guess I do live there, in that building." Jenny said.

The other girl laughed. "You mean you were sitting opposite your

own building and didn't know it? You sure are funny! I saw the moving van there. I saw you and your brother come out." She laughed harder.

"What's your name?" Jenny asked, amazed that she'd never seen this girl who'd seen her at least twice already.

"Rosa and yours?"

"Jenny."

"Do you want to play Jenny?" Rosa asked.

"Do you go out by yourself?" Jenny wondered.

"Sure, nobody is going to bother me. I have friends. You're alone yourself now aren't you?" Rosa looked up and down the street.

"Yes, but only by accident. My brother ran away from me. I've never been out by myself since I moved here."

"You're fooling me!" It was Rosa's turn to be amazed. "Well, you come with me. You've got to see some sights. Don't let your brother, what's his name . . . ?"

"Greg."

"Don't let old Greg the rotten egg spoil your good times." Rosa said and tore down the sidewalk.

Jenny ran after her. It was the first time she had run in the city. Rosa went in a different direction than Jenny and Greg had gone. She slowed down, when, at the end of the block, they came to another wide street.

"Rosa, what's that wonderful smell?" Jenny asked. She'd never smelled anything wonderful in the city.

"It's coming from there." Rosa said, leading Jenny to the front of a bakery. Whenever someone went in or out, the most wonderful sniff could be sniffed.

They sniffed cake and fresh bread and an indescribable sniff of everything good at once. But all the people rushing in and out knocked into Jenny and Rosa. So they left.

"The one bakery in town, in the country, did not smell as good as that bakery." Jenny said. "And you can't cook up a smell like that at home with one batch of cupcakes."

Rosa and Jenny went walking down the main wide street. Jenny hadn't been on such wide streets before now.

They were greeted by another fabulous smell. It was from a store that had cheeses and smoked fish and sausage and pickles. Rosa called the store a Deli, short for Delicatessen.

"Let's go in." Jenny sighed.

"I take you to see the sights and you just smell the smells." Rosa laughed.

Inside the Deli, they discovered the pickles floating in a big wooden barrel with a heavy lid. They lifted the lid a crack and whiffed the most fabulous whiff. Jenny was happy with one whiff. She was hopping with two whiffs. And Rosa whiffed with her.

"I'll get one of those pickles, girls, if you want." A woman said. Jenny and Rosa could hardly see her. She was hidden behind a row of sausages that hung from the ceiling, and a case of cheeses that stacked under the counter.

"We're just smelling them." Rosa said.

The woman raised her eyebrows and smiled.

"By the way, what does Delicatessen mean?" Jenny asked. She'd been very curious since Rosa used the word.

"It means the best eating." The woman put out her hands.

corned beef   1.50
roast be   1.75
choppe   1.10
tuna fi   1.10
roast tu   .90
egg salad

"We didn't have stores like that where I came from." Jenny said, when they were outside again.

"There are lot's more of them in the city. People from many countries come to America and live in the city. They cook their food in the old ways. They have stores that sell the kind of foods they need. Stores like Delicatessens and Bodegas."

"What's that?"

"Bodega? That's Spanish for grocery store."

"Do you speak Spanish?" Jenny asked, astonished again.

"Yes my parents speak Spanish as much as they speak English. They speak it to me all the time."

"How did they learn it, Rosa?"

"They were born in Puerto Rico. They learned Spanish as you learned English from the time you were a baby."

"Did they come from the country to the city then?" Jenny asked.

"Yes, many did. They have a good life now." Rosa said.

Jenny hoped she could have a good life too, if other people could.

"Will I learn Spanish Rosa?"

"Sure, you just did; Bodega . . ."

"Grocery store. Sounds like bow, they, ga, short a?" Jenny said.

"Right. There's one at the end of this block." Rosa pointed to a small store.

Out front Jenny saw many fruits and vegetables that were strange to her.

"These are all fruits that grow in southern countries, tropical fruits." Rosa explained. "Those green bananas are plantains. They get reddish later. You slice them and fry them like potatoes. It's sweet and fills you fast. Those are mangoes, the meat is sort of like peaches but more fantastic."

"I never thought I'd find new fruits and vegetables in the city." Jenny said.

"Now you're starting to see the sights, but I have a better idea. I'll

show you the whole city this afternoon." Rosa declared.

"But there isn't time, not in a hundred trillion jillion years!" Jenny cried.

"You'll see, now hurry." Rosa dashed away. Jenny chased after her.

The sun glinted low along the street. The traffic was shining so much Jenny didn't hear it booming. Her head whirled thinking how much city there was.

Running, they had enough speed to make their own breeze. Jenny flew. The sun bounced off the store windows. In a flash, Jenny glimpsed clothes and pans and toys and everything displayed in those windows. Rosa flew too.

With their last spurt of speed, they arrived at Jenny's street. They glided into Rosa's building. Rosa panted "I hate to wait for those creaky elevators, let's climb."

Stairs blurred into more stairs. Jenny scaled a city mountain of stairs. When there were no more stairs, Rosa scrambled up a narrow iron ladder.

"The super told us not to go up here"; Rosa said "But this is a special occasion."

"The super? Is that like superman?" Jenny asked.

"No, silly, the super of the building. He lives here and looks after it. He fixes and cleans and watches. In the city, your water and lobby and all belong to everybody. He takes care of what is ours." Rosa said. "Now, this way." And she disappeared through a small door at the top of the ladder.

Jenny was pleased that her lobby wasn't abandoned to spooks. She crawled up, out of the door onto the roof of Rosa's building.

"Here's the whole city." Rosa crowed.

Jenny could see buildings to the horizon. She felt like a bird. Rosa was talking.

Be careful at the edge. Over here is the river, that's east. The clump of trees is the park. There, south, that big round dome, is a place with a giant rock collection for everyone, a nature museum. Actually there's more of the city we can't see from here. But this is plenty for one afternoon."

"I love rocks. But that dome looks far. I'll never see it for real." Jenny said.

"You can go there by subway." Rosa said. "It's a fast train that runs underground all over the city. The bad part is that it makes too much noise."

"You don't like the noise either?" Jenny said, sure a city person had to enjoy noise to live in such a noisy place.

"I never get used to the noise. But I keep too busy to listen. And at night, I put a pillow over my head." Rosa said.

"I use a blanket." Jenny giggled. "But have you ever heard a bird? she asked, serious again.

"Sure I've heard a bird. By the river, we'll go some time." Rosa grinned.

"Does the city make you feel small and lonely?" Jenny looked out.

"No, there are just a lot of people like us out there. Life in the city isn't perfect of course." Rosa said.

"Life in the country wasn't either." Jenny was surprised to hear herself.

It was getting darker. Lights were twinkling and spreading over the city. Jenny felt like an astronaut looking down at earth. The building was her rocket. She thought how important it was to see something whole, far away, to understand it better.

"Rosa, did you say that was the park?" Jenny suddenly remembered Greg. "I better go, he won't find me here!"

"Wait a second Jenny, the first star." Rosa whispered, as if the star might hear and dim.

Jenny was happy to see the first star. But she did not wish. She knew she'd be making her own good luck soon.

"Now we better go before the super comes." Rosa said. "And so you can find Greg."

Jenny saw Greg sitting on the steps of their building.

"Where have you been!" he sniffled, glad and angry at once. "You weren't upstairs. I had to lie and say we were still playing and I just wanted some water and then I came here and I didn't know what to think."

"Neither did I when you left me." Jenny put her hands on her hips. She told him about Rosa. "I have a friend in the city now," she ended the whole story.

That night she lay listening to rain that had begun to fall. It splashed on the bricks and concrete outside with a sound louder and clearer than she'd ever heard. She was content resting in her dark room after all the smells and sights of the city.

A siren howled. When the noise died away the rain sounded even clearer. She put her plant on the ledge in the rain. In the lighted squares of other peoples' windows she saw other plants, tables, lamps. A man sat by one of the tables, a woman lit a lamp.

They were people like her.

Jenny was beginning to like the city. She liked shiny traffic and pickles. She liked looking out of windows and into windows. She liked meeting people around her and below her and next to her. She liked looking down from high buildings to see where she lived.

And the city could not stop the rain, or the stars.

THE END